# DANCING CRAZY

WRITTEN AND ILLUSTRATED BY

## Kathy Larson

# A White Turtle Books
## Grander's Reader

Written by and for grandparents
who read to their grandchildren

WhiteTurtleBooks.com

## Dancing Crazy

ISBN 978-1-933482-74-3
Library of Congress Control Number 2008935961

Illustrated by Kathleen A. Larson
Interior & cover design by Joel B. Reed

White Turtle Books
PO Box 2113
North Mankato, Minnesota 56002

*To Savvie, Jacks, and Carter*

My dad drove my mom to the hospital but she didn't look sick to me. She didn't have spots or a fever or anything.

My name is Jackson.
I have one brother and one sister.

One day we were all dancing crazy
and singing really loud.
My mom was laughing and laughing.

That's when my dad spoiled everything. He said, "Honey, you're going to the hospital!"

He looked worried, but I was mad.
Mom hardly ever acts goofy and we were
having fun.

Dad and Mom didn't leave until my gramma
and grampa came over.

"Let me think. Grandpa, where's Lily?

Peek-a-boo, Gramma!

Gramma started packing pajamas and clothes. My gramma's really nice, but she had this pretend smile on her face. I know that look. It means she's worrying about something but doesn't want me to know.

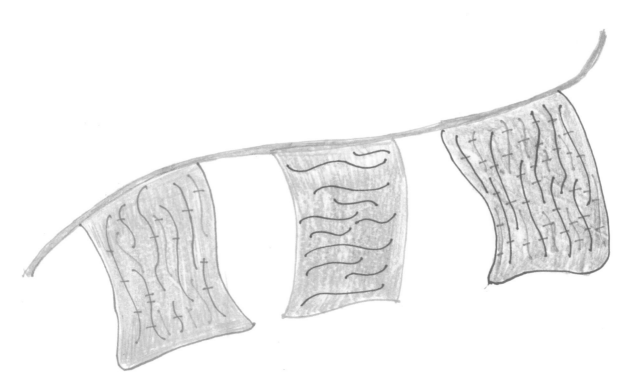

She said we were going to stay
overnight at her house, so I
grabbed all our blankets
and my stuffed dog, Rodman.

I gave Brooks
his Cougar and
made him carry
a couple of
Lillian's dolls.

I figured we might as well make the best of things.

Guys! I need you!

The next night my dad came back from the hospital and said we had to talk. Right away, I got scared.

Brooks said, "Where's Mom? Why didn't you bring her home?

I asked my dad if Mom had cancer but he said, "No, Jacks. She has Bipolar Disease."

Lots of pictures popped into my head...

polar bears...

the North Pole...

a barber pole...

but no "bipolar".

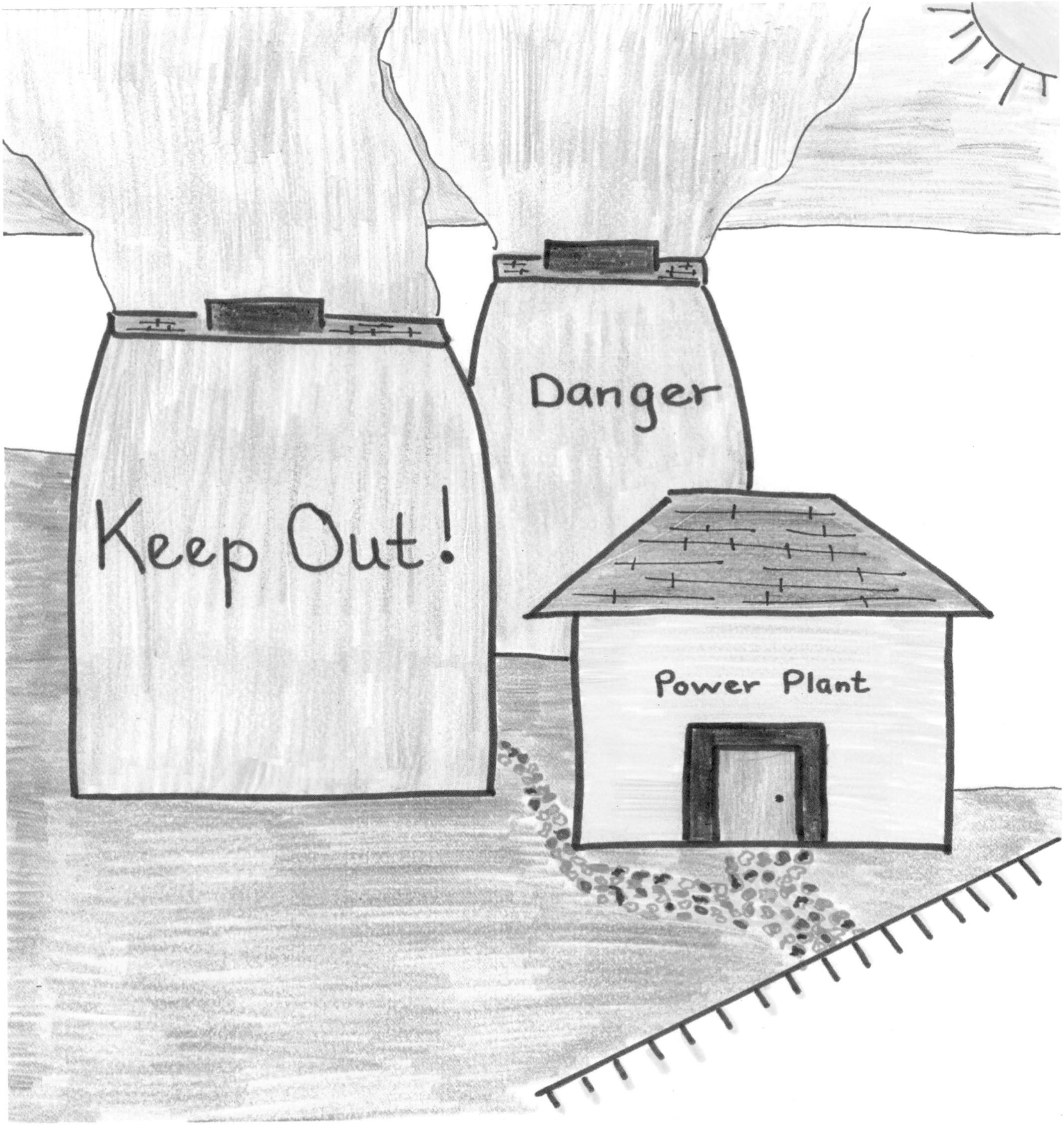
Danger
Keep Out!
Power Plant

Dad told me Bipolar Disease is a chemical imbalance in Mom's brain. I didn't really get what chemical meant, but he said it wasn't toxic chemistry like lawn fertilizer or a nuclear power plant. He said brain chemicals are more like table salt or Gramma's fake sugar.

With a chemical imbalance in her brain, Dad said Mom would have to stay in the hospital until the doctors figured everything out.

"Figuring it out" sounded pretty easy to me. If her brain's got an "imbalance", balance it. Put a cast on her neck so her head stays even. Or tell her she can't dance crazy again.

Ever.

But my dad said it wasn't that simple. He said the doctors would have to find the right medicine to make her brain "slow down". And we'd all have to make life better for mom.

Make life better for Mom?
Oh, sure.  I could guess what that means.

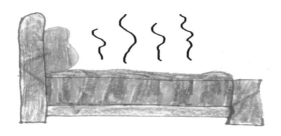

make my bed...

do the dishes....

do my homework....

Actually, it didn't sound too bad. I told Dad I could mostly do all of it myself until she got better.

But he said that wasn't good enough. He said, "Bipolar Disease lasts your whole life."

Do the math, Jacks.
70 more years...times 365 days...
times 3 meals...times five people?
It's not pretty.

Your whole life?   Now
THAT'S BAD!

So I slammed my books on the kitchen table and hollered.

"What do you mean she'll never get over it? Now what?

My word! Practice now? I have to start supper!

Who'll drive us to practice? Who has to cook? I'm not living at Gramma's for the rest of my life!

My dad just said, "Settle down. You're not living anywhere but right here. Mom will drive you to practice. And Mom will do the cooking."

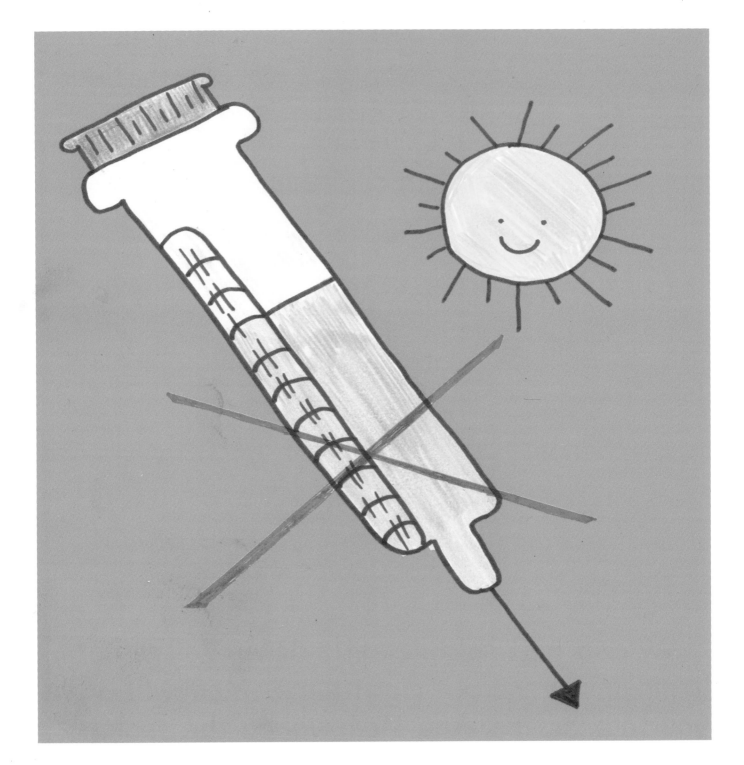

Bipolar Disease is kind of like Diabetes. My mom will always have it, but she won't always be sick. Instead of getting a shot every morning, she'll take her medicine every night.

It's called "managing the disease".

Sure, she might dance crazy again. Or sing really loud.

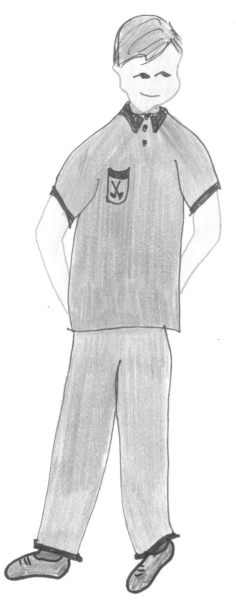

But if my mom starts to laugh and laugh, Dad will frown and call Gramma...

# About the Author

Kathleen A. Larson has spent her whole life helping children learn. As a schoolteacher for thirty-five years, she spent the latter part of her career in the challenging area of Special Education. Now retired, she spends her time as a devoted mother and grandmother, and writing stories for children with special needs and uncommon challenges. She makes her home with her extended family in Prior Lake, Minnesota.

LaVergne, TN USA
02 September 2009
156760LV00005B